B O O K R E V I E W S

Here's what people are saying:

Hissey's lovingly depicted toys are as gentle and unsentimental as her text. Old Bear, especially, is a threadbare treasure; the group drawing close in the joy of reunion makes a touching portrait.

from KIRKUS REVIEW

Sensitive, muted illustrations support this lovingly told tale.

from CHILDREN'S BOOK REVIEW SERVICE, INC.

Jane Hissey's first picture book has illustrations so finely detailed you can almost feel the worn, comfortable softness of the toys.

from PARENTS MAGAZINE

For Owen and Alison

This book is a presentation of Weekly Reader Books.
Weekly Reader Books offers book clubs for children
from preschool through high school. For further
information write to: **Weekly Reader Books,**
4343 Equity Drive, Columbus, Ohio 43228.

Published by arrangement with
Philomel Books, a member of
The Putnam Publishing Group.
Weekly Reader is a trademark of Field Publications.
Printed in the United States of America.

First published in the United States of America in 1986
by Philomel Books, a member of The Putnam Publishing Group,
51 Madison Avenue, New York, NY 10010. First published in 1986
by Hutchinson Children's Books, Ltd., London.
Printed and bound in Great Britain. All rights reserved.

Library of Congress Cataloging-in-Publication Data
Hissey, Jane.   Old Bear.
Summary: A group of toy animals try various
ways of rescuing Old Bear from the attic.
[1. Toys — Fiction] I. Title.
PZ7.H62701 1986 [E] 86-12227
ISBN 0-399-21401-1

Weekly Reader Children's Books Presents

Old Bear

JANE HISSEY

Philomel Books
New York

IT wasn't anybody's birthday, but Bramwell Brown
had a feeling that today was going to be a special
day. He was sitting thoughtfully on the windowsill
with his friends Duck, Rabbit and Little Bear when
he suddenly remembered that someone wasn't there
who should be.

A VERY long time ago, he had seen his good friend
Old Bear being packed away in a box. Then he
was taken up a ladder, through a trap door and into
the attic. The children were being too rough with
him and he needed somewhere safe to go for a while.

"HAS he been forgotten, do you think?" Bramwell asked his friends.

"I think he might have been," said Rabbit.

"Well," said Little Bear, "isn't it time he came back down with us? The children are older now and would look after him properly. Let's go and get him!"

"What a marvelous idea!" said Bramwell. "But how can we rescue him? It's a long way up to the attic and we haven't got a ladder."

"We could build a tower of blocks," suggested Little Bear.

Rabbit collected all the blocks and the others set about building the tower. It grew very tall, and Little Bear was just putting on the last block when the tower began to wobble.

"Look out!" he cried as the whole thing came tumbling down.

"Never mind," said Bramwell, helping Little Bear to his feet. "We'll just have to think of something else."

"LET'S try making *ourselves* into a tower," said Duck. "Good idea!" said Bramwell.

Little Bear climbed on top of Rabbit's head and Rabbit hopped onto Duck's beak. They stretched up as far as they could, but then Duck opened his beak to say something, Rabbit wobbled, and they all collapsed on top of Bramwell.

"Sorry," said Duck, "perhaps that wasn't a very good idea."

"Not one of your best," replied Bramwell from somewhere underneath the heap.

"I KNOW!" said Rabbit. "Let's try bouncing on the bed."

"Trust you to think of that," said Bramwell. "You never can resist a bit of bouncing, especially when it's not allowed."

Rabbit climbed on to the bed and began to bounce up and down. The others joined him. They bounced higher and higher but *still* they couldn't reach the trap door in the ceiling.

DUCK began to cry. "Oh dear," he sobbed. "What are we going to do now? We'll never be able to rescue Old Bear and he'll be stuck up there getting lonelier and lonelier for ever and ever."

"We mustn't give up," said Bramwell firmly. "Come on, Little Bear, you're good at ideas."

But Little Bear had already noticed the plant in the corner of the room.

"I've got it!" he cried. "I could climb up this plant, swing from the leaves, kick the trap door open and jump in!"

In case it wobbled, Bramwell Brown, Duck and Rabbit steadied the pot. Little Bear bravely climbed up the plant until he reached the very top leaf. He took hold of it and started to swing to and fro, but he swung so hard that the leaf broke and he went crashing down. Luckily, Bramwell Brown was right underneath to catch him in his paws.

"That was a rotten idea," said Little Bear.

"What I was thinking," said Duck, "was that it is a pity I can't fly very well, as I could have been quite a help."

"Ah ha!" said Bramwell. "That, my dear Duck, has given me a very good idea. I really think this one might work."

IN the corner of the playroom was a little wooden airplane with a propeller that went round and round.

"We could use this plane to get to the trap door," said Bramwell. "Rather dangerous, I know, but quite honestly I can't bear to think of Old Bear up there alone for a minute longer."

"I'll be pilot," said Rabbit, hopping up and down, making airplane noises.

"And I'll stand on the back and push the trap door open with my paintbrush," said Little Bear.

"But how will you get down?" asked Duck.

"I've already thought of that," said Bramwell, who hadn't really but quickly did. "They can use these handkerchiefs as parachutes and we'll catch them in a blanket."

BRAMWELL gave Little Bear two big handkerchiefs and a flashlight so he could see into the attic. Then he began to wind up the propeller of the plane. Rabbit and Little Bear climbed aboard and Bramwell began the countdown: "Five! Four! Three! Two! One! ZERO!"

They were off! The plane whizzed along the carpet and flew up into the air.

THE little plane flew beautifully and the first time they passed the trap door Little Bear was able to push the lid open with his paintbrush. Then Rabbit circled the plane again, this time very close to the hole. Little Bear grabbed the edge and with a mighty heave he pulled himself inside.

He got out his flashlight and looked around. The attic was very dark and quiet, full of boxes, old clothes and dust. He couldn't see Old Bear at all.

"Any bears in here?" he whispered, and stood still to listen.

From somewhere quite near he heard a muffled "Grrrrr," followed by, "Did somebody say something?" Little Bear moved a few things aside and there, propped up against a cardboard box and covered in dust, was Old Bear.

LITTLE Bear jumped up and down with excitement. "Old Bear! Old Bear! I've found Old Bear!" he shouted.

"So you have," said Old Bear.

"Have you been lonely?" asked Little Bear.

"Quite lonely," said Old Bear. "But I've been asleep a lot of the time."

"Well," said Little Bear kindly, "would you like to come back to the playroom with us now?"

"That would be lovely," replied Old Bear. "But how will we get down?"

"Don't worry about that," said Little Bear, "Bramwell has thought of everything. He's given us these handkerchiefs to use as parachutes."

"Good old Bramwell," said the old teddy. "I'm glad he didn't forget me." Old Bear stood up and shook the dust out of his fur and Little Bear helped him into his parachute. They went over to the hole in the ceiling.

"Ready," shouted Rabbit.

"Steady," shouted Duck.

"GO!" shouted Bramwell Brown.

The two bears leapt bravely from the hole in the ceiling. Their handkerchief parachutes opened out and they floated gently down . . . landing safely in the blanket.

"WELCOME home, Old Bear," said Bramwell
Brown, patting his friend on the back.
The others patted him too, just to make him feel
at home. "It's nice to have you back," they said.
"It's nice to *be* back," replied Old Bear.

T HAT night, when all the animals were tucked
in bed, Bramwell thought about the day's
adventures and looked at the others.

Rabbit was dreaming exciting dreams about
bouncing as high as an airplane.

Duck was dreaming that he could really fly and
was rescuing bears from all sorts of high places.

Little Bear was dreaming of all the interesting
things he had seen in the attic, and Old Bear was
dreaming about the good times he would have now
that he was back with his friends.

"I *knew* it was going to be a special day," said
Bramwell Brown to himself.